Also an OCTOPUS

or

A LITTLE BIT OF NOTHING

MAGGIE TOKUDA-HALL

illustrated by

BENJI DAVIES

WALKER BOOKS
AND SUBSIDIARIES
LONDON · BOSTON · SYDNEY · AUCKLAND

Every story starts the same way ...

with nothing. ───────────⟶

And every story needs a character.
Any character you can imagine!

Like a little girl.

Or an adorable bunny.

Or better yet ...

AN OCTOPUS!

An octopus who plays the ukulele.

But in order for it to be a story,
and not just an octopus,
that octopus needs to want something.

Like a sandwich.

Or a friend.

Or a totally awesome shining purple spaceship capable of intergalactic travel.

But that ukulele-playing octopus with intergalactic dreams can't just GET a shining purple spaceship, from, say, the corner shop.

And just why not?

That would be silly.

No, *you're* silly.

And also, that would make for a very short, very dull story.

For the story to be as totally awesome as a purple spaceship, the octopus has to earn it, by, say ...

BUILDING IT.
Out of fizzy pop cans and glue and string and umbrellas and glitter and waffles.

But what if the spaceship doesn't work?

THEN the octopus will try again,
but this time, with some help.

From an adorable bunny.

Ta-da!

Bunnies, while good friends, are not rocket scientists.

Not usually, anyway.

So the totally awesome spaceship
isn't totally awesome yet,
and it's certainly not capable
of intergalactic travel.

It's just a big mess.

By now, the octopus is starting to give up.

The octopus feels heartbroken.

As if the octopus will *never, ever* get on
a totally awesome shining purple spaceship
and fly to other galaxies.

So the octopus plays the ukulele,
because music is good for the heart.

But as the octopus plays, a strange thing happens:
the resolution to the story begins to take shape.

People come to listen to the
ukulele-playing octopus.

Friends. Strangers. Lots of people.

And a FEW of those people?
They're rocket scientists.

It's true.

Rocket scientists who don't just
build rocket ships — they also play
the saxophone, tambourine,
trumpet and lute!

So what happens next?

That's up to you.

When one story ends, it's just making room
for another story to begin.

And whether it's a story about a little girl,
an adorable bunny, an octopus,
rocket scientists or a band,
you've already got what it takes
to make that story whole.

Because every story starts
with the same thing:

just a little bit of nothing.

And everyone has a little bit of nothing!

It's true!

To my grandparents, storytellers all

M. T. H.

For Kasper and Lilly

B. D.

First published in Great Britain in 2017 by Walker Books Ltd
87 Vauxhall Walk, London SE11 5HJ

2 4 6 8 10 9 7 5 3

Text © 2016 Maggie Tokuda-Hall
Illustrations © 2016 Benji Davies

This book has been typeset in Agenda Medium

Printed in Italy by L.E.G.O. S.p.A.

British Library Cataloguing in Publication Data:
a catalogue record for this book is available from the British Library

ISBN 978-1-4063-6839-0 (hb)
ISBN 978-1-4063-7338-7 (pb)

www.walker.co.uk